I0788527

Special Thanks & Acknowledgements…

- ❖ To my One & Only Loving Sister, "My Support System Extraordinaire" - Linda Doris Jones-White (The baby out of 4 siblings who almost didn't make it here! Linda allows me to be who I am & supports me in every way necessary! Linda is also an author of 3 published books:

  > Fruit of the Spirit, Birthing by God's Supernatural, & Provision and Esther.

- ❖ My Dear Children ~ Jamie & Roxanne

- ❖ My Precious Grandchildren ~ Jamal, William & Destiny

- ❖ In Loving Memory ~ Of My 2 Brothers Walter & Ronald Jones

- ❖ All of My Nieces & Nephews & Greats definitely too many to name but Love you all!

- ❖ Special Friends Jacqueline V. Mayfield (Dr. V) & Shawn McLeod Encouraging & Believing in Me Always!

- ❖ To My Pastors ~ Lester & Rochelle Brown, Authentic Life Church, Philadelphia, PA

- ❖ Mercy Life of West Philadelphia ~ My Extended Senior Center Family

- ❖ Compassionate Women of Destiny & Women OF Compassion ~ My Women of Faith Sisterhood

- ❖ To my Publisher, Charlene Crawford for her commitment to complete my Dream into a Reality!

Passing the Baton through four Generations and Beyond

by

Carolyn Roberta Jones-Beard

Crawford
EDUCATION PLUS

Dedication

I dedicate my book to both of parents (deceased now) without them I would not be here!

Gone but never forgotten ... I love you & miss you both Mom & Dad ... Doris & Walter Jones!

Without both of you, there would be no generations to pass on too!

A special note to my Mother Doris Betty Jones a Virtuous Woman Proverbs 31:10-31 she was always there for me. Especially raising my children. I knew nothing thank God she was there she led by example.

Thank you, Mom!

TABLE OF CONTENTS

Chapter 1
In the beginning …

I wrote this book to encourage everyone to live your dreams to the fullest! It doesn't matter where you come from, where you begin and where you are now. When God has a plan for your life, it will come to pass. Jeremiah 29:11 says, "'**For I know the plans I have for you**,' declares the LORD, '**plans** to prosper **you** and not to harm **you, plans** to give **you** hope and a future.'"

This journey that I call life is not always easy. Expect and know that when you're going through your process, you will want to give up and quit! The pressure is real, strong and hard at times but know the end results will be worth it all! Just remember the responses become swift: "Do **not** be afraid nor dismayed because of this great multitude, for the **battle is not yours**, but God's. Position yourself, stand still and see the salvation of the Lord, who is with your always" (2 Chronicles

20:15).

Over 79 years of my life's journey, I get all my strength from "my God" (our relationship its personal), especially when I want to give up! I think sometimes nobody even notices that I try so hard! Then this verse comes to me from Galatians 6:9: "And let us **not** grow **weary** while **doing** good, for in due season we shall reap, if we **do not** lose heart." So, I continue to run the race God has given me "with patience and endurance," and I wait for the <u>winning</u> finish line results!

In life, there are so many distractions to keep us from winning, such as sickness and disease, attacks on your body and mind, financial distractions, job changes, the loss of a loved one and so many others, but we still can't stop! Remember delayed doesn't mean denied!

Just always remember that these things will make you stronger. Keep that determination and mindset, and realize that sometimes, depending on the days or hours, it seems harder than at other times, but that's what we do! Remember always that God is the "Doctor" above all doctors, and he is in full and total control of your life! Allow him to be your first go-to person in everything and in all situations that arise in your journey, which I call life!

My prayer is that as you read this book, it will allow you to lean and depend on God more and more!

Commit to a closer walk with him this day. Know him totally for yourself and watch what "HE" will do in your life when you give him the total surrender of your life!

My prayer is that as your read my book, chapter by chapter, that you will be encouraged, empowered and enlightened with a closer walk with my Personal Support System and Best Cheerleader: my Lord and Savior, Jesus Christ!

Chapter 2
Early Beginnings...

A beautiful, bouncing baby girl entered this world on October 8, 1941, at Philadelphia General Hospital (PGH) to the proud parents of Walter and Doris Jones. She was the second of two children at that time. Walter Jones III was born a year earlier on March 25th. The first girl, Carolyn Jones, arrived home in her parents' first apartment, which was at 8317 Lyons Avenue, at that time known as the Eastwick Section of Philadelphia (affectionately known as Elmwood), which was located near the Philadelphia Airport!

Our parents' journey was a great example of strength during this time. There were all levels the depression, civil rights and extreme racism. This could have given them an excuse not to lead by example, but they were true supporters of their children's life journeys and decision making.

They always led by example in their lives, even way back then. They taught us and showed us that no matter what life hands you, no matter what the color of your skin is, always reach for being the best you can be! Let nothing or no one stop you! Strive for the unreachable. They always taught us that success was the only option. We were to achieve and strive for more in life and to never settle for mediocre or for the status quo. They taught us to strive for the maximum in all we could do in life!

My dad showed us a strong work ethic by being a good financial support system, working diligently to help pay the bills and to keep a roof over our heads and food on our table. All needs were always met. Extras at that time were rare. This allowed us to learn that it was hard work to get ahead and that everything was not going to be given to us in real life. He felt also that we wouldn't have appreciated it otherwise if everything we wanted was always given to us.

My dad (Walter) worked at General Steel for numerous years at their first headquarters located in Eddystone, PA. Later, he transitioned when they moved out of state to Westinghouse, located in Lester, PA. Dad remained there for 35 years until retiring, and then he enjoyed retirement!

My mother (Doris) started in those days by doing housework, which was the only option in those days. Neither of my parents at that time had cars, so we walked and took public transportation. That was it! So, as I reflect over those days and those precious memories, I never forgot the struggles, the hard times and the sacrifices she made for us. As you know, there is nothing like a mother's love! I remember how my mom would take us every day, no matter what the weather was. It could be rain, shine, snow, sleet, hail, just like the mailman. Mommy would put us in the "red wagon" and literally pull us all the way to Miss Mary an hour each day and each way!

How I loved it during the rides. She would sing to us hymns of praise, gospel songs and share stories about God's love and goodness. Mom would tell us how much God loved us and the sacrifices made just for me. "Don't you ever forget that!" she'd say. I didn't, and I brought my children up in that same way. It was a lesson well learned that should be passed on from generation to generation!

Mom never once complained. She did what she had to do to survive and to provide for her children. Many times, she did this without food for herself and some necessities as well! Then she would walk to the bus stop after dropping us off and take transportation to work. Mommy would work all day long cleaning other people's houses, doing floors on her knees, cooking, taking care of their kids and so much more! And then she'd come back to Miss Mary's to get us with the red wagon, put us all in it again and walk another hour home with more singing, laughter, rhymes and riddles! It was so much fun, and we learned so much from her without even realizing it!

Once home, Mom did her housework and home responsibilities, such as feeding us, bathing us, preparing meals for us and the household breakfast, lunch, dinner and snacks. Then bedtime for all! After all that, she'd get herself ready and go to bed for a few hours of rest and then wake up early every morning and start all over again, day in and day out and weekends too!

Mommy would never complain, realizing she was preparing her children for greatness! My mother, Doris Betty Jones, was that virtuous woman in the Bible! …

… Proverbs 31:10-31-King James Version
[10] Who can find a virtuous woman? For her price is far above rubies.
[11] The heart of her husband doth safely trust in her, so that he shall have no need of spoil.

[12] She will do him good and not evil all the days of her life.

[13] She seeketh wool, and flax, and worketh willingly with her hands.

[14] She is like the merchants' ships; she bringeth her food from afar.

¹⁵ She riseth also while it is yet night, and giveth meat to her household, and a portion to her maidens.

¹⁶ She considereth a field, and buyeth it: with the fruit of her hands she planteth a vineyard.

¹⁷ She girdeth her loins with strength, and strengtheneth her arms.

¹⁸ She perceiveth that her merchandise is good: her candle goeth not out by night.

¹⁹ She layeth her hands to the spindle, and her hands hold the distaff.

²⁰ She stretcheth out her hand to the poor; yea, she reacheth forth her hands to the needy.

²¹ She is not afraid of the snow for her household: for all her household are clothed with scarlet.

²² She maketh herself coverings of tapestry; her clothing is silk and purple.

²³ Her husband is known in the gates, when he sitteth among the elders of the land.

²⁴ She maketh fine linen, and selleth it; and delivereth girdles unto the merchant.

²⁵ Strength and honour are her clothing; and she shall rejoice in time to come.

26 She openeth her mouth with wisdom; and in her tongue is the law of kindness.

27 She looketh well to the ways of her household, and eateth not the bread of idleness.

28 Her children arise up, and call her blessed; her husband also, and he praiseth her.

29 Many daughters have done virtuously, but thou excellest them all.

30 Favour is deceitful, and beauty is vain: but a woman that feareth the LORD, she shall be praised.

31 Give her of the fruit of her hands; and let her own works praise her in the gates.

I thank God every day for my mom's strength, persistence, patience and the legacy she left to me! Her godly training allows me to be the woman of God I am today!

Proverbs 22:6 New King James Version SAYS…

Train up a child in the way he should go, and when he is old he will not depart from it.

This is the example MOM gave to us for her entire lifetime! Precious memories—how they linger in me forever!

A few years later, my brother Ronald Jones was born June21st! Now there were two boys and myself as the only girl! During that time, my dad got his license and bought a car. Still the days continued the same. Ronnie was added to the red wagon too! Day in and day out, mom walked, sang and pulled the wagon to meet the immediate needs of the household.

Survival but wanting more was always my mom's desire! At that time, Mom's ultimate dream was to become a nurse. She never gave up on that dream. She did the process of life continually by taking care of all three children at this time and meeting her husband needs as well.

Mommy was still striving to do what she wanted most out of life for herself. Sometimes not with much support at home; she still continued to press and cry out to her God for strength and direction on how his plans for her life would come into her life and make her happier and more successful in her life's journey.

I thank God every day for her strong Christian upbringing from her mother and my grandmother, which was passed on to my mom, where her faith would never fail as she continued through all her life struggles and never gave up! Then her pressures began to get even harder, but she still couldn't stop. She continued be an example and role model to her kids and her grandchildren while she lived until her passing.

Sometimes, I listen to my daughter Roxanne talk about things she and her grandmother talked about regarding her life, and they did come to pass. And even 40+ years later, she still talks about the witty suggestions and tidbits she gave. The blessing is now Roxanne tells the stories to her children about their great grandmother. This is what I mean and why it's so important about being able to pass your legacy and baton to your children and their children and beyond, never to be forgotten!

She continued along with everything else going on in her life, being wife, mother and so much more to others. Mom continued to persevere through God to reach another level in him for her and her family.

Leading by example, she went to beauty school Venus one of the first black at that time. She was a trendsetter way back then; it's amazing!

She did everything it took to make it happen. Of course, there were times she wanted to quit, but she never did. The stakes were too high!

She pushed through extra longs days and nights, needing those late hours to study and prepare, but she never slacked in any of her other daily responsibilities of taking care of her family. She received her license and became a licensed beautician!

After graduating, she was able to stop doing housework and started doing women's hair in a beauty shop. She worked all types of hours around her daily routine, but she kept persevering and bringing more money in for her family in the process of life.

But unfortunately, after several successful years in hairdressing, she started having major issues with her throat. This came from the very harsh chemicals being used during that time. Her doctor informed her that she could not do it much longer. If she continued, it would affect her talking and she would eventually lose her vocal cords. She continued to work a little longer while preparing for the unforeseen transition. So, shifting again, she pushed and went back to school one more time!

During this time, she decided to ultimately pursue her dream for nursing school and again she was determined to succeed, and she did! My mom was a very independent African American woman who never gave up! With extreme circumstances, she beat all the odds and persevered through any obstacle that tried to stop her.

Doris Betty Jones achieved her degree as an LPN licensed practical nurse at the top of her class! Praise God for what he has done.

Her ultimate dream and goal were achieved, what she once thought would be impossible, but it came to pass. She would say to us, "Always remember this during your life's journey …"

Matthew 19:26 *New International Version*
"With *man* this is *impossible, but* with *God all things* are *possible*." I remember this as one of mom's favorite scripture and saying it all the time she lived by it all her life!

After thinking that life was good and things were falling into place quite nicely, big life changes happened again! My parents had to move from Eastwick. A new development came in, which is now called "New Philadelphia." It surrounds the Philadelphia Airport vicinity. They had to relocate, and they purchased a new home in Yeadon, PA, in 1960. This too was another milestone for several reasons.

One, they were the first African American family on the block and in that area. At this time, Mommy was so blessed to pass her driver's test. She received her license and purchased herself a brand-new car and surprised Daddy with all of it!

Shortly thereafter, not feeling very well, she went to her family doctor, believing she had a tumor. Well shockingly enough, Dr. Douglass called her to come into his office. Dr. Douglass said, "It is not a tumor; it is something entirely better. You are about to have a baby!" She could not believe it. At age 42, the doctor had to be wrong! When she went home and told her husband, he was first shocked then quickly changed to being happy and proud of the bragging rights for his age!

So needless to say, just 6½ months later, and still in total disbelief, when Ron, her third child was graduating from John Bartram High School in South West Philadelphia, just 2 weeks later, Linda Doris Jones, a 4-lb preemie, was born, starting a brand-new chapter for both of my parents.

Mom and Dad now had a new home and a new baby! Their lives changed drastically in their older years. I believe they were thinking freedom with no children left at home, but this was not God's plan! It was a total new beginning!

Chapter 3
Living My Legacy by Passing the Baton through four Generations and Beyond

I have lived through four generations and beyond, beginning with my grandparents, Jefferson and Betty Cook; my parents, Walter and Doris Jones; my siblings, Walter, Carolyn, Ronald and Linda; and now the children, grandchildren and great grandchildren (of all the siblings) It's a slew of them!

WOW, now that's an awesome life testimony in itself and a precious gift from God to me! The blessings of God will keep in my mind always, remembering those years near and far. These precious memories will linger for a lifetime. Remember at all times where you came from and where God is taking you. Realize and recognize it's only through God and not yourself!

I would never think of doing this book on my own. But God is my forerunner, source and sustainer. I had an awesome support team who continued to help me set goals, create a vision and make new visions to help me reach my final destiny in the completion of my book. Never forget where you came from and where God will take you to and the blessings that come along the way! I am so blessed!

Growing up as a teenager is another step in my life's journey…new challenges, new expectations and so much more. This was not always easy, but only the strong survive! Another step in my life journey was the changes of new schools, new friends, and new homes, and I survived it all. Changes come with life. The journey was and is always real! Life is a journey and the choice is up to you what path you choose to take. The most important thing is to keep God in the forefront of all your decisions and choices. Don't get caught up in what others say and do. It is not always the best way to make choices and can lead you to a path of destruction and heartaches.

The first experience for me and my brothers was catching public transportation once we were old enough. Our new home was not far from the Philadelphia Airport area. It was very hard to get adjusted with both of our parents working a lot to provide us with all the things we needed and a few wants occasionally. We were on our own a lot, but we made it! We lived with strict rules and knew not to break them. We knew what we could do and what we could not do. All the siblings were raised the same way when it came to the rules of the house. There were no exceptions! "You live in my house, you go by my rules!" Our parents' words were final, and there were no options! The main #1 rule in our parents' house was that you were taught God first and foremost! You went to church every Sunday all day, no exceptions, and we never missed!

Our routine as we got older was very different, but we adjusted again to the new routine. We would go to school together on the trolley. After school, we would all come straight home together, and then we were responsible for doing our homework. We were assigned weekly chores and we stayed in the house when my parents were not home. When Momma returned home, we had to be ready for updates on our day, homework checks, chores completed and then it was time for dinner and then cleaning up and putting away all the dishes.

After dinner, we had a little fun time and then off to a set bed time of 7pm daily, no options. I remember when we would be looking out our bedroom windows while watching the other neighbor children playing outside, but not us. Those were the house rules, no exceptions!

On occasion, we could go out on a Saturday, and before the street lights came on, we had to be in the house, no exceptions. That was all three of us at that time. Education was a rule in the house, and we had to be promoted every year. None of us were ever left down a grade nor went to jail! "Be the best you can be" was always reiterated, and "never let your dreams not come to pass!"

I remember in my adolescent years that these words were very important in preparing me for my future. Thank God for the people in my life during those times who helped me on my journey. So many people helped me to move on, giving me directions and encouragement along the way. They were my teachers in school and Sunday school, my church leaders, members and so many friends in our church and family. In those days, if you did something wrong, no matter where, if an adult was there and saw you, they had full reign to correct you on the spot, and then when I got home, I would get reprimanded again by my parents.

We had excellent role models back in the day, and they actually led by examples. They walked the walk and they talked the talk. They had true character. Everyone doesn't have that today! That's truly missing in some of the generations, as well as respect, values and knowing the difference between right and wrong. Even when it came to just simple manners. We always had to address an adult with Mr. or Mrs. Nowadays, kids call adults by their first name. I think it's awful! What is this world coming to?

I am so thankful and blessed at 79 years old that I grew up when I did. The upbringing really means a lot! I am still able to teach, show and lead by example for others of all ages and stages of what God can and will do by living by his Word and His life's principles! I still say old school was the best school in teaching right and wrong in our children and the old traditions!

I have no regrets. My childhood allowed me to become who and what I am today. I am a strong African American Woman of God, a powerful prayer warrior and woman to be reckoned with! I realize that now, but I didn't always back then. I was a work in progress! God's masterplan in the making!

I feel this is missing a lot today. Many of my childhood friends were raised with less restrictions and had more flexibility and they could basically do whatever they wanted to do. Many of them died early or were in jail and so much more. Also, the girls had baby/babies out of wedlock, which of course was not an option back then in our house. No way, not in the JONES HOUSE.

So, when the first three siblings turned 17 and had graduated high school, we all left for our freedom, but we realized really fast what real life on your own really meant! Paying bills and household responsibilities and so much more—what a change! At home with our parents, there were rules but no bills!

The preparation was at times really tough, which allowed us to be fully prepared for what I call "LIFE." I thank God for the training that kept us and prepared us for real life! I think about all the times and remember the upbringing. We were taught God first, family second and your job last.

We were all brought up being raised in our family church, which was First Baptist Church of Paschall, in Southwest Philadelphia. It is still there today. From time to time I get a chance to visit.

It's fun to go and remember the good times and the relationships that were built that remain near and dear to my heart. I have a lifetime of precious memories! I remember staying in church all day until sometimes late afternoon and sometimes until late at night and then finally going home. Again, the rules were the rules, and they did not change! I must say that we did also receive much love, nurturing and training along the way. That was the key. There wasn't much money in those days, but we did not know it. We did not lack anything that was necessary! Love was the key and should still be today (not buying materialistic stuff). We had very little but turned out very well, all of us! Most of all, we learned how to be very independent!

When going back and forth on school days, I remember learning to go different ways to school and taking various transportation, never knowing what might occur and never having to be stranded due to unforeseen circumstances that could arise any given day.

We loved riding the trolley but never rode the 11 trolley much. Our new school, Tilden Jr. High School, was at 66th & Elmwood Avenue. I am so thankful that my older brother, Walter, who went to school with me, took really good care of me and taught me the do's and don'ts. Our everyday routine on school day was get up, get ready for school, get breakfast, get your bagged lunch, go catch the trolley.

After school, we returned home, changed out of our school clothes, did homework and chores. Shortly thereafter, our parents would be home. On Saturdays, if our parents were not home, we'd have breakfast and clean up house. We'd stay in; if it was a nice weather day, we could go out in the backyard only. We were not allowed to go out of the yard under any circumstances.

Our church activities increased as we grew up. I remember so well BTU (Baptist Training Union), Children's Church, Youth Committee, Children's Choir, Jr. Ushers and eventually continuing as a young lady and still growing in Adult Sunday School, Adult Ushers, Senior Choir, Sunday School Teacher, ADA B. Lemon Pulpit Guild and eventually Church Secretary at First Baptist Church of Paschall for Rev. Khalfani Drummer. Thank God for those years! The memories are so dear, precious and limitless for me.

A moment to remember and mention in the life of First Baptist Church of Paschall, which I will remember forever involved the chairman of our Deacon Board at that time, W. Wilson Goode.

During his entire run for mayor and election, it was simply incredible! He grew up as a child at First

Baptist Church of Paschall. My brother Walter and Wilson graduated from Bartram together and of we all lived our lives at FBCP. It was awesome to help with his campaign, and when he won, we all went down to the Philadelphia Convention Center for his victory speech. We had special seating of course, and it was truly amazing to be a part of his election process, from the beginning to the end! In good and bad we all stood together as a family, no matter what!

I thank God for those years and for being able to grow up with those fond memories. I would not be who I am without the upbringing and guidance of my FBCP. The growing up process was not always an easy one. As I reflect, I even grew up in some of the times during segregation and racism. That was horrible! It's so different for me now somewhat. Even when it comes to the stores, doctor's offices and more now having bars on their windows, having to lock our doors, we never used to have to do that, but now we're locking everything up. I have learned this with my new home. The process was long but it was great. Waiting for God to show up and show out with greatness!

Family and friends are always so very important to me. I remember my co-workers while I was working in the laundry at Delaware County Memorial Hospital. This is where Mrs. Brown introduced me to the love of my life! I remember Momma and the words she taught me. When on a date, meet at a place where there are many people around you just in case! So, a couple of my co-workers went along with us, and I knew all things worked together for good for those who love the Lord. This too was a learning experience from God where he was ordering my steps and preparing me for what was coming forth next in my life's journey. I continued to work hard, attend church on a regular basis and do the right things.

During that time, I began teaching my new friend how to travel around the City of Philadelphia. By this time, I was grown and living in my very own new apartment. My first experience of real life living in the City of Philadelphia. This was definitely an adventure in itself for me! Luther, who at that time was a very dear friend of mine, was living in Villanova and worked at Villanova University for numerous years.

In a very short time, a love connection was made with the true love of my life. We dated only four short months and eloped, marrying in Elkton, MD, at the Justice of Peace. This is when the love developed more and more and our life story did too! What a beautiful life we shared for 45 years of marriage! From this union, we were blessed to raise and nurture two loving and supportive children, Jamie Luther Beard and Roxanne Lynn Beard. This was only the very beginning as being older parents.

I thank God for the numerous steps which he allowed us throughout our small beginnings! We lived for many years over a pharmacy on Main Street, Darby, PA. Neither of us ever drove a car using only public transportation all of our lives. Living My Legacy by Passing the Baton Through Four Generations and Beyond allows me to see the entire picture and to be a part of it all from the beginning to the very end. This tells my story, my parents' and my grandparents' lifeline. This has been a way to share and also allow me to pass this book on to others, especially to my family and special friends. This is a way to pass on some of the good traditions shared by our generations and to inspire the next generations to do the same by reaching for the impossible! Don't ever settle for mediocre.

When I look back over my life, I think of the precious times I had with a very special friend to our family, Sis. Novella Brown (now deceased) who was a member of First Baptist Church of Paschall, Philadelphia. Sis. Brown was very influential in helping me get my employment at Delaware County Memorial Hospital in Drexel Hill, PA. She was a great and powerful Woman of God, and a great supporter to my oldest son Jamie; she was his godmother. They had a special bond, and on birthdays and holidays, Jamie never forgot to spend time with her, especially in later years when she was in her 80s and 90s. She was always surprised on his pop-up visits. It was always short and sweet. She would call me about how she loved him so and was so very proud of him. She'd watch him as he left her house until she couldn't see him anymore going to the bus stop. I always taught Jamie and Roxanne never to forget those who were there for you always!

As my children became older, we rented a house from her in Darby, PA, and lived there through there finishing high school years. Thank God to the very end she was an intricate part of our entire family. I remember especially after the death of our mom—they were very close, and that's how we became so close to her and to her children and their family members.

The cute story of how Mom and Ms. Brown met and then became lifelong family and friends to the end went like this: At the birth of my baby sister, Linda, they were in Philadelphia General Hospital at the same time. It was affectionately known back then as PGH. It was also so amazing that the last person my mom saw before her passing was Sis. Brown; she prayed with Mom at her bedside, and Mom shouted all the way through her prayer! Little did we know Mom was in her process of going home to be with her Lord and Savior Jesus Christ! By the time we returned from taking Sis. Brown home, Mom had left us and went to be with the Lord; she was still warm! She was not alone. Thank God our prayers were answered. She would not have wanted it any other way. Kevin, her son-In-law (whom she always said was her son) was with her until the very end. He always supported her.

Mommy lived with Kevin and Linda for her last seven years. It's truly amazing how God does what he does! When I now travel past Mrs. Brown's house, I think about her and the important memories we created and she left behind! I remember Christmas holidays. In her later years, in her 80s and all through her 90s, Sis. Brown would cook for us.

Year after year, she insisted, "As long as I can do it, I will," and she did it! We looked forward to the holidays because of the old-time tradition being continued. It reminded us of how we used to celebrate the holidays, the good old days with Mom, Dad, children, and grandchildren. We would laugh in her home, sing praise and worship and holiday songs, and eat loads of food. Her specialties were glazed ham, fried chicken, golden brown turkey with homemade stuffing and gravy, sweet potatoes, macaroni and cheese, mash potatoes and gravy. Her roast beef would melt in your mouth, and of course we loved all her homemade desserts, not limited to the most delicious hot apple and sweet potato pie and of course her favorite coffee ice cream. We would eat, sleep, wake up and start again. We would be there until early hours the next morning! Reminiscing of the good old days gone but never forgotten! The holidays are just not the same anymore. Many of the traditions are lost and so are the family ties, which was more important than the gift giving!

The younger generation have no clue of what they are missing! I always love and remember Grandma, Grandpa, Mom, Dad, Walter

(Sonny), and Ronald (Ron) who are gone from this life but the lasting memories are for a lifetime!

After moving to another level in life, starting late in life and having and raising my family was a true-life awakening experience! I thank God for my mama. I really knew absolutely nothing about being a mom! The blessing was she was a nurse and a mom of four, and she helped me learn so much! With both of my children, I had a caesarian section. I didn't even know what that was or what that entailed. My son was a difficult birthing process, and God knew what I had to go through during that pregnancy. My daughter's birth process was even more difficult! He covered me through it all, and today at age 79, I am still a survivor!

I had to stop working after the birth of my son Jamie. "To much is given much is required." Thank God for my strict, Christian upbringing. It taught to continue pressing without stopping! For a long period of time, I traveled back and forth with my mom, driving Jamie to his preschool, training and preparing him for his next level of education to come in Media, PA. As he continued his educational journey, he moved onward and upward, preparing for the transition of his new school where he would be riding the yellow school

bus and later graduating from William Penn
School District.

There were tough times, which I call life,
but it was well worth it all when Jamie received his
diploma! I am so proud of Jamie, who lives with
me now. He worked at Dunkin Donuts for ten
years and now works at UPS coming up soon to 20
years. He has received numerous awards and
employee of the month and various other
certificates from them as well.

Anyone who knows Jamie knows he is a
very quiet unassuming but loving and caring man
who loves his Mama (me!) with all his heart, soul,
mind and being! It shows when you see us
together, and the great care he gives me. We go out
for weekly rides to the store. I cherish our mother-
and-son times. Jamie is now such a blessing to me
in my latter years living with me. Words cannot
express my gratitude!

I remember when my son Jamie was born;
we lived in a small apartment on 10th Street in
Darby, PA. Two years later, Roxanne was born; it
was another total life-changing experience! I thank
God we both survived! My daughter was even
more difficult; I woke up 2 days after the birth to
see my precious baby girl! My blood pressure

raised so high we both were almost lost during that delivery. They gave me so much medication to get it down. I was asleep for two days straight after the delivery, but God covered me through it all. Even as of today, I am still a survivor at 79 years of age! Roxanne was a blessing also from God.

After our second child, Roxanne, I had to go back to work and help my husband to provide for our two children and their needs. It was a huge struggle because neither my husband nor I made a lot of money, but we did an honest living and the best we could for them, sacrificing ourselves most of the time so they would have what was needed. Two paychecks are always better than one, no matter how small! Later it was all well worth it!

I remember many times eagerly awaiting for Luther to come home in the evening. He'd travel on several buses to get home from Villanova to our home then in Darby, PA. He would work the morning schedule every day. His routine started like clockwork around six in the morning to be ready for the first bus to start around 7:30am. Then I would prepare to go to daycare by 8:30am, then on my way to work at 9am and then having to be at work at 10am. WOW, what a morning! I always thanked God for traveling mercies each day for both of us to and fro, but especially my husband;

God's grace and mercy kept him safe! God knows the thoughts and plans of good and not evil for that expected end (Jeremiah 29:11).

I thank God for early beginnings. There were times when I was the only one working part-time, so massive struggles, but it allowed me to get to where I am today. The growth of God is amazing in our lives! Not knowing what he's doing but knowing he knows and it's only the best for his children! He makes no mistakes ever and is not a liar; isn't that good to know? Being able to stand on his Word sustained me during the hard times and the challenges knowing he would never leave me or forsake me. At times, he carried me through the process! Later in life, we moved to 339 N. 10th St. Darby, PA.

I remember it was a corner house; it was a little bigger with more space, a closed in porch and a larger Bedroom. It had an enclosed back yard for the children to play! This was a blessing, and the children grew up in one bedroom. We were able to buy bunk beds for them to sleep on. Luther and I slept on a pull-out sofa bed in the living room. We did this for many years.

It is such a blessing to see our children grow up and develop into little people, then teenage years and now adults with their own families and stories. It's a lifetime of changes for both us and them! What a difference a day makes! Most of their education was in the William Penn School District. Roxanne went to Park Lane School from kindergarten to 6th grade. Next, she went to Evans Elementary School, Bailey Rd, Yeadon, PA.

They lived in many places, but God continued to do so many things, and he knew what he was doing in our lives. Thank you for allowing me to survive through it all! I thank God for allowing me and my husband Luther to travel to many places and to do many things before we had children. A few of our memorable trips I will never forget were with First Baptist Church of Parshall. Deacon Theodore Thompson ran a trip ever year. To name just a few, we went to Puerto Rico several times, Bahamas, St. Thomas, Cancun, and Canada. We enjoyed flying, cruising—all of it!

Those were such great fun times and so many memories! Now I can't travel far like I used to, but I just reminisce often looking at the pictures too! Once again as I look back over my life, it's been God's grace and mercy that has allowed me total joy and happiness throughout it all!

I remember Mama's teachings and spiritual guidance in all things! First Baptist Church of Paschall, thank you for leadership, rules, regulations, the by-laws and more. There is nothing like old school doctrine, and it still stays in me today. I share with the younger generation because some of it is definitely still worth sharing for their benefit in this day and time!

Chapter 4
Reflections on My Why

My Spiritual Walk which has been my church life. This lifeline helps you understand why I am who I am today. As a lifelong member for 60 years what a great experience! I call it my Family Church and that's what it was! We all loved, cared, shared with each other in gladness and sadness! We were an awesome support system with each other. We were a true family for so many years and still today. The learning, teaching, preaching & nurturing of God's Word allowed me to grow and develop into who God wanted me to be today! My grandparents, my parents and even some of my aunts, uncles and cousins went there too.

I was so blessed to have sat under the tutelage all five of the previous pastors during my sixty years!   Rev. William H. Lemon, Rev. William Jones, Rev. Samuel L. Taylor, Rev. Randolph Bracy and Rev. Khalfani Drummer. There was also an Interim pastor during the time Rev. Bracy left and
Rev. Drummer came aboard who I loved which was Rev. Edward Grant. All of these were awesome men of God who left an indelible mark

on my Christian Journey which can never be erased!

Then God moved me to Impacting Your World Christian Center for ten years under the Leadership of Pastors Ray & Tracey Barnard. A whole new level and dimension going from a Traditional Baptist Church to a Non-Denomination Church. There teachings were amazing! Totally new and different. I must admit they grew and stretched me to a whole new level in Christ!

After that new level of increase God moved me again to Authentic Life Church, Philadelphia under the Leadership of Pastors Lester & Rochelle Brown. It's been going on 7 years and a true awakening for me to be so blessed by much younger pastors and their new way of bring God's Word to me and ideas have taken me even higher in my spiritual growth process with the Lord! New directions, in sites and more by just being obedient and listening to God's voice and knowing when to move when "He" says so!

Thanking God still for my precious memories which will never be forgotten moving on family members deceased at this time are: Truly missed the Love of my Life my very Loving & Supportive Husband of 45 years before his passing

Luther Beard. By this union we have 2 children who both are so attentive and supportive in my older years, Jamie Beard & Roxanne Beard-Carroll, Eric Carroll Husband, My 3 Grandchildren who I am blessed to have to been here for each of coming in to their world deliveries … and seeing them growing up through adults … Jamal, William & Destiny. My many friends at Mercy Life Center West Philadelphia, My Dearest baby sister Linda D. Jones-White & Kevin L. White my Brother in Law.

Our Women's Ministry Compassionate Women of Destiny Global Ministries, Inc. We started together my sister Linda and I from the ground up in September 2005, given by God and all praises for this year we are celebrating 15 years of service to Women in unfortunate life situations & circumstances needing a helping hand and an encouraging word.

In conclusion all I can say … Although missing my Luther now for five years being with the Lord I have learned to be content abase or abound…lonely sometimes yes butThe Bible clearly teaches us to "be content" no matter what our circumstances are. In **Philippians 4:11**, Paul said, I have learned in whatsoever state I am in therewith to be content. The Amplified Bible describes being content as satisfied to the point where you are not disturbed or disquieted. It doesn't say satisfied to the point where you don't want change, but satisfied for now until God brings the change.

I truly enjoy my God time! Staying in Gods Words as long as I want and growing higher and higher in Him. I am truly living my best days now! The Lord has given me the desires of my heart… **Psalms 37:4 reads- Delight thyself also in the LORD; and he shall give thee the desires of thine heart**. I also made this a commitment of mine and God showed up & showed out every time in my life! … Psalms 37:5 - Commit thy way unto the LORD; trust also in him; and he shall bring [it] to pass.

I now live for my Lord & Savior Jesus Christ! I am now a Minister of the Gospel, being ordained in August 2015 in Oaks, PA, by Rev. Dr. Nancy Gamble a True Sister in Christ and a Powerful Minister of the Gospel in her own rite! Rev. Dr. Gamble is a Board Member of Compassionate Women of Destiny Global Ministries Inc.

As the Overseer over the Wholeness & Wellness Outreach Ministries. This Ministry is under the Umbrella of CWODGM, Inc. which services goes our Nursing Homes, Hospitals as well as supporting Shelters, Halfway Houses, Homeless Initiatives and Domestic Violence in the City of Philadelphia & variety of counties in Pennsylvania and Delaware.

I am an Encourager that's my purpose in life now! Wherever my team and I can go and give a word and a helping hand that's what we do! Unfortunately, we have not been able to do as much recently since the pandemic but preparing for the upcoming winter season and into the upcoming 2021 new year and new season. Trusting in new expectations and new beginnings!

To God Be the Glory for the things He Has Done! It's not me but the God in me! I live to serve and to help others whenever and wherever I can! I don't want or need accolades or titles. I have a heart for the people!

Living and Leaving My Legacy which is …

If I can assist somebody along the way, then my life was worth living!

Chapter 5
Fulfilling My Dream …

Thank you, God, for allowing me to fulfill the dream given by you, for me, to complete my first book by my 79th birthday on October 8, 2020. To God be the glory for the things he has done! Here it is …*Living My Legacy by Passing the Baton Through Four Generations and Beyond.*

I have been truly blessed beyond measures to have lived through all four generations and beyond! What a privilege and an honor to have been chosen by my Lord and Savior Jesus Christ to have completed this assignment of "HIS" for my life!

I thank and praise God for the opportunity of being chosen to be stretched, and yes, I was totally stretched out of my comfort zone! To have been able with God to have achieved this amazing level of success and at my age is truly unbelievable!

Anyone who knows me knows one of my favorite scriptures, which I quote all the time, is, **"To** whom **much is given,** from him **much** will be **required"** (Luke 12:48). This is definitely true!

As I reflect on my life and the many seasons I have been through, so many times I have had to pray and meditate on Ecclesiastes 3:1, and I use this as my life's confirmation, which says, "To everything there is a season a time for every purpose under heaven." I am extremely grateful to God for allowing me to have the strength, patience, and endurance to complete this task! All of HIM and none of me! I take no credit. It's all about HIM always!

I must admit some of the pressures and the persistence were somedays harder than others, but I thank God most of all for the silent moments we shared together often. During these times, it allowed me to push and endure to the end consistently and constantly!
Psalms 30:5 says, "Weeping may endure for a night but joy cometh in the morning." That **verse represents** for me that you might have to cry for a while, but when you've been through the crying, there will be much <u>joy</u>! So, the weeping for me was well worth it all when the end results of that joy were my unspeakable "joy" that only God can give!

I would hope and pray that this book would inspire and be an inspiration to so many and allow you to see and realize, not to make excuses about your age. Age really does not matter! Age is only a number! You are never too old or young to be used by God!

Here I am a living witness at age 79 that I have been truly blessed to have written and published my first book. I fixed my mind on Jesus! Lord, you are so faithful to me! So many thoughts fill my mind:
"WOW, I feel like I am in a dream."
"Is this really true?"
"Look what God has done for me!"

I feel and believe that God showers blessings on me more than anyone else! I am a true and living testimony of God and of how he uses us for his purpose and plan at any age. I've written my first book at age 79! Hallelujah, it's God's grace and mercy. The best is still yet to come in my senior season of life!